Anna The Farting L

Dizu Fizu Press

Rhymes: Darren Hughes

Illustrations: Aria Jones

Did you hear
About the famous llama?
Who shot to fame,
After all the drama.

Anna was her name,
And she had a strange rumbly tum.
But she was famous,
For what came out of her bum.

Anna loved beans,
And ate them all the time.
But the smell it made
Could have been a crime!

One friend - Alex
Didn't mind the smell.
Although at her back end
He tried not to dwell.

They both loved to
dream
Of the craziest things.
Like flying up to Jupiter,
If Anna sprouted wings.

Or swimming to the titanic,
To walk down the great staircase.
Then challenge the mermaids
To an epic relay race.

Alex whispered;
So you and I couldn't hear.
They collected all the beans
That were somewhere near.

Anna jumped in,
Like an Olympic swimmer.
Then ate every bean
Leaving no room for dinner.

They packed a suitcase,
Fitting in an extra tin.
Anna tried to fart,
"No, you gotta keep it in!"

"I have a better idea" replied Alex,
After stroking his chin.
"Every fart that comes out,
We'll put another bean in?"

Then they left the house
And tried to get on the bus.
But had to get off quite quickly,
When the farting caused a fuss.

They managed to stop a cab,
Luckily the driver had no sense of smell.
"Head north, please" said Anna,
As they waved the house farewell.

The driver left the city.
They noticed something on the dash
He had an open tin of beans -
Along with his very own stash.

Anna and Alex quickly learned,
All about their taxi cab driver.
Henry was his name,
An old-time war survivor.

They finally arrived
At their chosen location.
Black Rock Desert, Nevada.
Full of beans and expectation.

A lady called Jessi was there,
With a twin jet-powered car.
Apparently, it goes very fast,
But not very far.

They lined up at the start line,
Anna started to feel scared.
Alex jumped on her back,
"FART POWER!" he declared.

The race began,
And Jessi pulled off strong.
But Anna started farting,
So the race didn't last long.

Anna flew past Jessi,
Leaving behind a green fog.
Breaking the land speed record,
Using the power of a smelly smog.

This is the end of their story,
Anna and Alex are back home.
But now, they travel fart
powered,
Whenever they do roam!

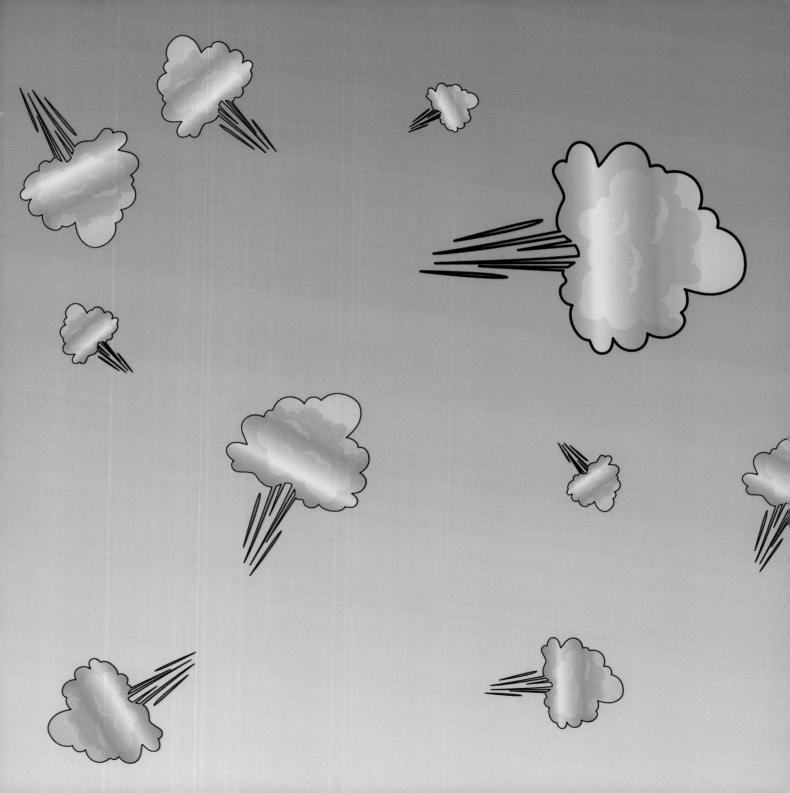

Printed in Great Britain
by Amazon

79557550R00018